PETE FROM PLUTO
AND
HIS PERFECT PIES

Lorraine Piddington

Grosvenor House
Publishing Limited

The right of Lorraine Piddington to be identified as the author of this
work has been asserted in accordance with Section 78
of the Copyright, Designs and Patents Act 1988

The book cover picture is copyright to Lorraine Piddington

This book is published by
Grosvenor House Publishing Ltd
Link House
140 The Broadway, Tolworth, Surrey, KT6 7HT.
www.grosvenorhousepublishing.co.uk

A CIP record for this book
is available from the British Library

ISBN 978-1-78623-950-1

For Zachary, Isaac, Barnaby and pie eaters everywhere!

Pete from Pluto makes many perfect pies,
Fat, thin, big or small, he makes them any size.

He fills them to the top with many different things,
Sometimes cheese or vegetables, sometimes with
    small herrings!

Then Pete covers them with pastry, rolled out to
   perfection
And bakes with care, this delicious pie selection.

When golden brown he puts them on his window shelf
   to cool,
The freshly baked aroma can be smelt for miles by all!

Pete eats pies in the garden, the kitchen and the park.
He eats them in the daytime and even in the dark!

He makes pies for his friends when they come round
   to tea
And takes pies on his boat when he goes out to sea!

He shares them with the fish, the crabs and lobsters too,
Often hungry seagulls swoop down to steal a few!

Daring Pirate Pam heard about Pete's perfect pies
And decided to send out some sneaky pirate spies!

She desperately wanted to taste Pete's pies for herself,
When the smell of freshly baked pies wafted out from
   his window shelf.

So the pirate spies crept up to Pete's house on tippy
   toes,
Then stole some perfect pies from right under his nose!

Clumsily stuffing them inside their raggy baggy
   clothes.
But Pete looked out, and gave a shout, so they quickly
   hid and froze!

Then they hurried away as fast as they could,
All the way into the dark, wild wood!

Pete was puzzled and thought, 'Where did those pies go?'

He scratched his head, frowning and searched high and low.

But Pete's friend Fred from planet Fop
Had seen the antics of this lot!

But was too far away to stop the pirates bold
Who had taken the pies as they were told,

By daring captain Pam, who was eager to taste
Those pies being brought to her with bumbling haste.

Fred from Fop was going to tell Pete
About what he had seen from his garden seat;

Whilst watching his favourite pets play,
On this warm and sunny day.

Biltonion biscuit monsters so happy and cute,
Running around with Fred's old boot.

Eating biscuits, their favourite food,
Which always put them in a good mood.

Meanwhile, those puffed out pirates had stopped to
 rest,
Breathless Pearl said, 'I can't go on, I've done my best!'

Unfortunately, a pie fell out from under Pearl's hat,
And slim Jim said, 'Well fancy that!'

Pirate Phil said, 'We can't sit any more,
Our pirate boat is anchored offshore!'

'So let's hurry back to Captain Pam and the crew,
She'd be cross with us resting if she knew!'

They rushed to the ship laden with pies,
Captain shouted, 'Welcome back my pirate spies!'

'I see you have Pluto Pete's pies for us to try!'
But a flock of seagulls were circling in the sky

Watching the pirates place the pies on the table,
They suddenly flew down as quick as they were able

And took the perfect pies from the pirate ship,
Held in their beaks with the strongest grip!

By now Pluto Pete and Fred from Fop
Had arrived at this very spot!

They jumped aboard ship as quick as a wink!
And said 'Something has gone on here we think!'

'Yo ho, we think NOT!' said the pirate crew!
Pete noticed the pie crumbs and knew!

'Come on!' said Pete, 'Stop telling lies!'
'You can't pull the wool over my eyes!'

Fred from Fop witnessed the scene
Of you pirates being mean!!

Stealing pies from my window shelves
To eat them all for yourselves!!'

'Seagulls flew off with them high in the sky,
So we didn't get to taste one single pie!'

Said Captain Pam with a heavy sigh
Then pirate Jim began to cry!

'We are sorry!' They all sadly said to Pete,
Who was so kind, he arranged a special treat!

He took the pirates home with dearest friend Fred,
And made them lots of perfect pies from recipes in
   his head.

They played games, sang songs and had such fun,

All the pies were eaten and the clearing up was done.

The pirates all agreed never again to spy or steal,
They would often pop to Pluto Pete's for a perfect pie
    meal.

Helping him with his shopping, his gardening and
    cleaning too,
They scrubbed and cleaned his pie tins, and made them
    shine like new.

Pluto Pete, Fred from Fop, the biscuit monsters too,

Were now firm friends with Captain Pam and her pirate crew!

Lightning Source UK Ltd.
Milton Keynes UK
UKHW050253290920
370677UK00006B/223